ISBN 978-1-948898-06-5

Library of Congress Control Number: 2021942825

Designed by Jaclyn Sinquett

Edited by Emma D. Dryden

Printed in Canada

10 9 8 7 6 5 4

by
Shannon Anderson

Pictures by
Jaclyn Sinquett

FEEDING MINDS PRESS
American Farm Bureau Foundation for Agriculture®

To my mom, who survived my unwavering determination over the years.
— S.A.

For my dad, the master gardener.
— J.S.

April 5

I LOVE strawberries!

I love them so much I could eat them **every day.**

scratch & smell

"Mom, can I grow strawberries of my very own?

"That's a lot of work, Jolie. Maybe when you're older."

"*Looking* older isn't the same as *being* older, Jolie."

April 10

Mission #2: Act Older

I need to act like an old person. I'm going to act like mom + dad. They're always making food and cleaning the house, so I'm going to feed Munchy and clean his cage all by myself.

munchy →

Mission #4:
Keep grass <u>alive</u>.

April 15

I just watered my grass seeds.
I'm keeping them in my window
so they get lots of sun.

April 17

Mission Update: It's Alive!

YAY! Little baby sprouts!

I showed my grass to Munchy.
He tried to eat it, so I think
that's a good sign.

Mom and Dad are even impressed.

"If your grass keeps growing,
you'll have to start mowing."

Old people are funny.

April 21
Mi$$ion #6:
Make Money

I wanted to show Mom how old I can be. I did **all** the watering. (That way Mom could rest. OLD PEOPLE need rest, right?)

When I was in the yard, I noticed the Franklins were having a garage sale.

Wait a minute, that's it!

GOTTA GO!

"Hey, Mom! Can I set up a lemonade stand?"

April 22

Mission Update:
SUCCESS!

I sold lemonade for **3** whole hours yesterday. I made **$6.00**!
I only sold two cups—one to Mrs. Franklin and one to Grandpa—but Grandpa gave me a whole **FIVE DOLLARS** and said

"keep the change."

That's a big tip!

I'm sure I've got enough money to buy strawberry plants now.

草莓
(Chinese)

"Jolie, you've been helping out a lot and showing you want to be responsible.

We can try planting strawberries if you take care of them *and* harvest them all by yourself."

"YES! Thank you! I'll be the best planter and picker you ever saw!"

April 26

The plants are so cute with their little white flowers. I can't wait to harvest them! I have to grow them first, though.

cute →

"*Harvest* means to pick the strawberries when they're ready."

May 5

Breaking News!

Tiny green strawberries are starting to grow!

 hi

hey

May 10

strawberry update:

BIRD ATTACK!

Going onto high alert!

"I'm watching you, you strawberry-stealers!"

May 25

I had enough strawberries today to fill a **whole cup!**

Did you know strawberries have their seeds on the **outside?**

Seeds right here! →

So juicy

May 29

Way more strawberries today! If this keeps happening, maybe I can make a **pie!** YUMMM

"Looks like you have enough for ten pies, Jo!"

June 5

Guess what we had for breakfast?

strawberry pancakes!

jordgubbe (Swedish)

we

were

goooood

It's a good thing school's out because my strawberries are going **bonkers!** I have to pick them *every day.*

"Let's freeze some so they don't spoil."

"Then we can eat strawberries all winter. Yum!"

"Munchy, don't tell Mom and Dad, but...
I'm so glad it's raining!"

June 18

I don't have to pick strawberries today. **Phew!**

June 20

My berries _loved_ the rain. Either that or I must be the best strawberry farmer ever.

There's a <u>bazillion</u> of them!

Did you know that parts of strawberry plants grow long enough to bend down and plant themselves to make **more plants?** I didn't either.

BONUS PLANT!

Runners

"Jo, there aren't enough berries left to have the stand again."

June 30

I think the patch is getting tired. zzz I know I am!

I may have to let the birds eat the rest.

"Mom…"

First Time Planting Strawberry Plants

Strawberry plants come in three different varieties: June-bearing, everbearing, and day-neutral. The difference between the plant varieties is identified by when and for how long each produces strawberries during a growing season.

The strawberries Jolie plants in this book are a June-bearer variety called Earliglow and are designed to produce fruit early in the growing season. June-bearers are the best fit for a home garden. In most locations in the United States, June-bearers produce buds in the fall, then flower and produce fruit in June. They also produce runners in the summer.

In the first year of growth, it's best to pick off the blossoms so the flowers don't turn into fruits. This allows the strawberry plants to focus on developing healthy roots and give you a more abundant strawberry harvest in their second year.

For a typical first harvest, strawberries might not produce as much fruit as Jolie's plants do. In real life, it can take a year or more to produce such a big crop. You can check out your state's Cooperative Extension program to find information about growing strawberries in your state. Search the name of your state, followed by the words "extension strawberries," and you should find some great information.

Source: https://www.almanac.com/plant/strawberries

Integrated Pest Management

What do you do when a bird tries to attack your garden at home? A pest is an unwanted plant or animal that can damage crops and spread disease. Farmers use a strategy called Integrated Pest Management which helps prevent their crops from damaging pests.

Farmers try to do this in the safest way for people, pets, and the environment. For example, ladybugs can be introduced to a crop to eat pests called aphids. Netting or fencing might keep larger animals out. Pulling weeds from a garden is even part of a smart Integrated Pest Management plan. Sometimes chemicals can be used on crops to prevent pests; if used, you should always let an adult handle the chemicals and always follow directions on the label to make sure they are safely used.

U-Pick

At a U-Pick or Pick-Your-Own farm, it's fun to pick your own berries, pumpkins, flowers, and more! Farms have rules in place for U-Pick customers to follow. Some examples of these rules include safety precautions, such as customers not being allowed to go into areas with farm equipment or other potentially dangerous locations. There are signs in place identifying which crop a customer can or cannot pick to ensure the crops that need more time to mature aren't picked too early. Check out your state's tourism or visitor's bureau to find local U-Pick farms in your area.

Farmers charge a fair price for their crops to honor the hard work and time spent producing the crop. The pick-your-own price also includes the value and unique experience a customer gets from picking their own products.

Sources: https://extension.tennessee.edu/publications/documents/pb1802.pdf

For **free educational activities**
and videos visit: www.feedingmindspress.org

The goal of **FEEDING MINDS PRESS** is to
create and publish **accurate** and **engaging books**
about **agriculture.**